Duff's Monkey Business

Illustrations by Kim LaFave

FIRST NOVELS
The New Series

Formac Publishing Company Limited
Halifax, Nova Scotia

Formac Publishing Company Limited acknowledges the support
of the Cultural Affairs Section, of the Nova Scotia Department
of Tourism and Culture. We acknowledge the financial support
of the Government of Canada through the Book Publishing
Industry Development Program (BPIDP) for our publishing
activities. We acknowledge the support of the Canada Council
for the Arts for our publishing program.

Canadian Cataloguing in Publication Data

Wilson, Budge

Duff's monkey business

　(First novels. The new series)

　ISBN 0-88780-498-5 (pbk.)
　ISBN 0-88780-499-3 (bound)

I. LaFave, Kim.　　II. Title.　　III. Series.

PS8595.I5813D843 2000　　jC813".54　C99-950277-8
PZ7.W69004Du 2000

Formac Publishing
Company Limited
5502 Atlantic Street
Halifax, NS B3H 1G4

Distributed in the U.S. by
Orca Book Publishers
P.O. Box 468 Custer, WA
U.S.A. 98240-0468

Printed and bound in Canada.

Table of Contents

To my friend
Marie Milton Davis

1
Discovery

It was May the twenty-second. Duff Dooley lay on his bed and listened to the traffic on Clonsilla Avenue. A bus screeched to a stop half a block away, and he could hear men laughing and the click of high heels. It was time for him to get up.

In about six weeks time, he was thinking, the summer holidays would begin, and then he could get up earlier or later — whatever he felt like.

Then he and Simon Abrams could go to Hasting Park for a softball game with the other kids. Or play with their Frisbees, or just lie in the grass talking. Better still, they could go to Jackson's Park and look for stranded pirates, or maybe search for discarded flying saucers and stray elephants in the picnic area.

Duff grinned when he thought about those special crazy adventures. Only yesterday his father had said that he and Simon had too much imagination for their own good. He didn't seem to realize how much fun it was to dream up things that weren't really there.

But today was a school

day, so Duff jumped out of
bed and put on his clothes —
including the red shirt that
his mother said clashed with
his hair and freckles. He
could hear bacon sizzling on
the kitchen stove, and he was
hungry. He took the stairs
two at a time, and plopped
himself down at the kitchen
table.

"Ready," he announced to
his mother, holding out his
plate.

His mom kissed him on
the top of his untidy red hair.

"Feed the cats, first," she
said, "and it wouldn't do your
hair any harm if you put a
comb through it."

Duff went out to their huge
garage, which had once been

a barn when the city had been smaller. Long ago, their home had been a farmhouse, with cows in the barn and chickens in the backyard. Duff liked to think about those days.

He opened the big barn door, and called the cats. The garage was full of junk, as well as a lot of useful things like tools and bicycles and spare flower pots and lawn chairs — everything except a car. "Not worth protecting that old car," Mr. Dooley would say. "And the millennium will have long gone before we can afford a new one."

When the cats didn't come running for their food, Duff

looked around. Then he stopped as suddenly as if he'd been lassoed.

There was a monkey sitting on top of their old rocking chair.

This was scary. It was also pretty exciting

Duff dashed into the house. "Mom! Dad!" he yelled. "There's a monkey in the barn!"

"There he goes again!" laughed Mrs. Dooley, and his father grinned.

"Boa constrictors yesterday. Monkeys today," he said. "And probably a couple of international spies tomorrow." Then he frowned.

"Duff. Hurry. Feed those cats and get back in here for

your breakfast. School starts in fifteen minutes. Lucky for you it isn't far away." When Duff returned to the barn, the monkey was still sitting on the rocking chair.

"Hi, monkey," whispered Duff, as he filled the cats dishes and put them outside. "Please, monkey, be here when I get back from school. Simon'll come too. We'll bring you some supper. And I'll give you a name."

The monkey scratched his chest and his stomach. His long tail reached down to the floor. He seemed to be listening to what Duff was saying. Maybe he wasn't so scary after all.

"Bye, monkey," said Duff,

and closed the door behind him very carefully.

When Duff got to the school yard, he called out to all the kids, "Hey, guys! Listen! Guess what! There's a monkey in our barn!"

"Gimme a break!" growled one of the big boys in grade six. "That kid is something else. Last week it was a sea-serpent in Little Lake. Now it's a monkey in the barn."

"But there is. There really is!" insisted Duff. He went over to Simon, who was hanging upside down on the jungle gym. "After school," he whispered. "Over at my house. You'll see!"

2
Simon meets Mulligan

When school started, Duff could hardly wait for silent-reading period. He knew exactly which book he would choose. On top of the tallest bookcase was *Jungle Animals and Their Way of Life*. Surely this book would tell him what monkeys ate. He had to know — and fast.

"Monkeys eat tropical birds and tropical leaves and bananas," he read. Well, bananas he could manage. He had eight dollars saved for a new Titan hockey stick, and winter was a long way off.

During show-and-tell, Duff tried again. "Mrs. Huppman," he began, "today I found a monkey in the barn."

"Duff," said Mrs. Huppman patiently. "You know the rules. You show and you tell about real things. Save your monkey for tomorrow's story time. It might make a very interesting story about pretend things. Loretta — it's your turn. What have you brought?"

Duff scowled as Loretta showed the class a huge doll with yellow curly hair. "Girls!" he muttered to Simon. "Wait'll they see the monkey! That'll open their eyes."

At noon, there was a music-festival practice. Duff did not

know how he could live
through singing the same
song seven times, over and
over and over. However, he
did live, and after a while it
was three o'clock and the
school bell rang.

Duff and Simon dashed
down to the One Stop Store
and bought some bananas.

Mrs. Dooley watched the
boys as they came in the
kitchen. "What's in the big
bag?" she asked, as she
spread peanut butter on their
sandwiches.

"Oh, you know," said Duff,
between mouthfuls of bread.
"Stuff for the monkey."

Mrs. Dooley was used to
Duff's bags of stuff.
Yesterday she'd found a bag

containing nine chestnuts, four speckled rocks, two elastic bands, a pigeon feather, a padlock, nine pine cones, twenty-two hockey cards and a stubby pencil.

When Duff and Simon went out to the barn, the monkey wasn't on the rocking chair.

"Aw, Duff," complained Simon. "I thought you really meant it this time."

"I did. *I did*!" snapped Duff. But he was worried. "Maybe he found the old stove hole, and just left." Leaving me with two dollars worth of bananas, he thought.

Suddenly Duff yelled, "Mulligan!" He had the name all ready. He'd been saving it

for something special.

There — up above — was the monkey, hanging by his long fingers from one of the high beams. Simon looked up. "Awesome!" he whispered. "*Awesome*!"

Duff laid a banana on the rocking chair. Swinging from rafter to rafter, jumping on soft noiseless feet, Mulligan leapt down onto the chair and gobbled up the banana. Then he jumped up and down, squealing.

"I know exactly what he's saying," said Duff. "He's saying, 'More! More! More!'" He gave him two more bananas, and the boys watched as he held the second banana daintily with

the long, long skinny fingers
of one hand, and thoughtfully
scratched his head with the
other.

Later, when they went
back in the house, Duff's
mom asked, "Where on earth
have you two been for so
long? It's almost supper time."

"Outside in the barn, of
course," said Duff. "With the
monkey."

"Yes, dear," said Mrs.
Dooley, smiling, "of course.
In the barn with the monkey."
Then she added, "And now,
off you go, Simon. I think
your mother's a little bit
worried."

3
Monkey in the dark

That evening, after dark, Mr. Dooley came up to Duff while he was counting his hockey cards. "Duff," he said, "will you please go out to the barn and get my screwdriver for me."

Duff thought about the dark old barn and Mulligan's beady little eyes. "Lookit, Dad," he said, "can I get it for you first thing in the morning?"

"No" said his father. "I need it now. Right this minute. One of the light sockets is broken, and your mom needs the light for her sewing. Why not now?" Mr. Dooley was frowning.

"Because of the monkey," mumbled Duff, looking hard at his hockeycards. "He's not a bit scary in the daytime, but it's really dark tonight. He's big, and I don't know him all that well, yet."

Mr. Dooley wasn't amused. "There may be a time and a place for your monsters and your space creatures," he said sharply, "and your monkeys. But this isn't it. Out you go, young man, and bring me that screwdriver."

Duff went. He coughed loudly as he entered the barn, so that Mulligan would hear

him coming, and not be
frightened into doing
something crazy — *like*

jumping down on his head.
He swung the flashlight around nervously until he found the screwdriver. From up above he could hear low chattering noises.

Grabbing the screwdriver off the rack on the wall, Duff ran towards the door as fast as he could go, tripping over the old rocking chair. He fell flat on his stomach, but he hardly even felt it. He arrived back in the kitchen panting, with his eyes large and round.

"See him?" grinned his father, who was feeling friendly again.

"No," heaved Duff. "But I sure could hear him."

"Sure," said his father, as he took the screwdriver. "Thanks."

4
Problems

The next week was an exciting one for Duff and Simon. They spent part of every day in the barn with Mulligan, teaching him new tricks, and watching his wonderful gymnastic leaps and swings. They talked about him constantly at home and at school.

Duff's sister would roll her eyes and say, "Oh, sure." The teacher would plead, "Oh come now, Duff!" or "Please, Simon." Their friends kept saying, "Yeah. Yeah. Tell us another one."

At first Duff and Simon didn't mind that no one believed them. They were having too much fun to care. And they were used to telling stories that they knew no one would believe — about space-men hiding in Sears, or rattle-snakes in the girls' locker room.

But as time passed, the kids found life becoming more and more difficult. Duff's mother started to get concerned about him. His father became more and more impatient; he had problems at work that were enough to worry about. His sister didn't like admitting to her friends that it was her brother who was "seeing monkeys."

Mrs. Dooley asked her doctor if he thought Duff was really healthy and normal. She suggested that he be given tests. Secretly, Mr. Dooley went to the church and talked to the priest. What do you do when your son tells lies all the time?

Whenever Duff and Simon took people to the barn to meet Mulligan, the monkey hid in the rafters and kept very quiet. Only when they were alone did he come down and join his friends.

At school, the kindly and patient Mrs. Huppman became impatient and less kindly. She said she might speak to the principal if they didn't confine their stories to story time.

When Duff or Simon began to talk about Mulligan, the other kids started growling, "Oh shut up! Boring! Boring!" Then they'd throw their Frisbees to everyone except the two boys.

So, little by little, Duff's monkey became a burden to them. They loved him, fed him, played with him. They made chattering noises and hung upside down from the branches. But they stopped talking about him.

They also got tired of seeing their allowances disappear on the day they got them. They could hardly

stand the sight of a banana.
They picked up old pop
bottles to make money. They
robbed their piggy banks.
And that wasn't all. Duff had
to spend one whole Saturday
morning at the doctor's
office, answering questions.
Simon's mother went to the
synagogue half an hour early
one week, in order to speak
to the rabbi. The Dooleys'
priest gave two homilies in a
row on the wickedness of
lying.

After a while, everyone
started to get short-tempered
— the Dooleys, Simon's
parents, the teacher, the boys
themselves — even Mulligan.
Some of the anxiety seemed
to be rubbing off on him.

So everyone was glad to hear that the circus was coming to town. Most people enjoy circuses — even doctors and priests and rabbis and teachers and parents. Duff and Simon could hardly wait to see the Monkey Act. Maybe they could learn some new tricks to teach Mulligan.

Of course the other kids had lots to say, such as, "Tomorrow you'll be seeing *real* monkeys, eh, Duff?"

Mrs. Dooley said to her husband, "Maybe if he sees the circus monkeys, he'll stop pretending he can see one in the barn. I hope so. It's really starting to get on my nerves."

Mr. Dooley patted her knee and said, "There, there dear."

Secretly he thought, "Drat that boy for worrying his mother!"

5
Chee-Chaw

The circus was a great
success. The night of the
show was pleasant and warm.
Inside the enormous tent, the
seats rose almost to the roof,
and everyone seemed to be
eating popcorn and cotton
candy and laughing and
shouting.

Finally, the bugles and
drums announced the start of
the performance, and the
clowns came tumbling in,
dressed in baggy pants and
flapping shoes, with huge
painted grins.

The audience gasped and squealed as the trapeze artist flew through the air, catching the bar at just the right moment. The lions did their tricks without gobbling up the trainer; and girls in pink tights did terrifying things on the backs of racing white horses. The bears roller-skated and somersaulted, and the tightrope walker breezed across the rope as if it were as wide as a sidewalk.

At last it was time for the Monkey Act. Duff's sister Eileen dug him in the ribs, and he and Simon leaned forward on their seats.

Out they marched — a little troupe of monkeys

dressed in red coats, with tiny Mountie hats on their heads.

When they reached the centre of the ring, the trainer stood up on a stool. He had a shiny bald head and a huge black moustache. He bowed four times, and then raised his hand for silence.

Then, through the microphone, he made this announcement:

"Ladeez and gennulmen! My name is Mr. Antonio and I am pleased to present my famous Mountie Monkey Act. It will be good! It will be great! But I have to apologize. There may be a few small imperfections in our performance. Three and a half weeks ago, when we

were passing very close to this town, our lead monkey — our wonderful Chee-Chaw — escaped from his cage. He completely disappeared. The other monkeys need him for leadership. He was like a little monkey general."

Here the trainer took out a large checkered handkerchief and wiped his eyes. Then he raised both arms and shouted, "But the show must go on! And believe me, it will be good!"

Simon and Duff looked at one another. Simon's eyes looked as big and as round as billiard balls. Mrs. Dooley looked at Mr. Dooley, and the two of them looked across the aisle at the Abrams. Over in the opposite bleachers, Mrs. Huppman looked at Mr. Huppman, and the principal looked at both of them. The priest looked at the rabbi, and the doctor looked at everyone. And all over the stands, children were looking at one another, their mouths wide open.

The trainer yelled, "Showtime!" but nothing happened for a moment. Then he called "Showtime!" again, and finally a monkey in a fancy gold trimmed jacket dropped down from high in the rigging. Then the monkeys marched forward to begin their act.

Afterwards, almost no one who knew Duff and Simon

could remember one single thing about the Mountie Monkey Act. At the end of the performance, Mr. Dooley turned to Duff and placed his hands gently on his shoulders.

"Duff," he said. "Listen carefully. This is very important. Is this monkey-business of yours one of your pretend stories? *Or do you really have a monkey in the barn?*"

"Yes, Dad, I do," said Duff. "And now I guess we all know that he didn't just drop out of the sky or arrive straight from Africa."

As people started leaving the tent, many of them — the kids, teachers, the doctor, the priest, the rabbi — looked

over to where Duff and
Simon were standing. Some
of them waved. Then they
smiled sheepishly and looked
down at their feet.

6
Showtime!

The Dooleys and Abrams
waited until the crowd had
left the tent. Then they all
went down to the trailer
marked "*Mr. Antonio*" and
knocked on the door.

The monkey trainer was
dressed in a long red
nightshirt. He didn't look one
bit pleased about being
disturbed. He grunted and
frowned at them.

Mr. Dooley spoke first.
"I'm sorry to bother you at
this hour, but we think we

may have your missing monkey."

Gone was the big frown. A broad smile lit up the trainer's happy face.

"I can't believe it!" he shouted, throwing open the door. "This three weeks without Chee-Chaw has been like a nightmare for me. Two years I spend training that monkey — my little Chee-Chaw — and then, POOF! he is gone. Quick! Take me to Chee-Chaw so we can make a reunion. I'm so excited I'm almost dying!"

"Hold on a second," said Mr. Dooley. "We have to make sure it's the right monkey. Would a circus monkey be so shy that when

strangers appeared he'd hide in the rafters of a barn and not make a single sound? The only ones who've seen him are these two boys."

"Oh, ho!" cried Mr. Antonio. "That's my Chee-Chaw. He's trained to stay hidden in the tent rigging until I shout, 'Showtime!' Then he drops down for everyone to see. Come! Where is this barn? I will show you." He hauled on his trousers and stuffed his nightshirt inside.

So all the Dooleys and Abrams went along to the Dooleys' barn, even though it was very late and very dark.

When they went inside, Mr. Antonio turned on his flashlight. The monkey was

nowhere to be seen. Then the trainer yelled, "Showtime!" Suddenly Chee-Chaw swung into view with a happy shriek, and landed on his trainer's shoulder.

Then Mrs. Dooley invited everyone into the house to celebrate with lemonade and chocolate chip cookies. Mr. and Mrs. Dooley and Eileen and Mr. and Mrs. Abrams said, "I'm sorry" to Duff and Simon. Duff and Simon said, "I'm sorry" to Mr. Antonio. He laughed a big booming laugh. "Sorry!" he cried. "For what are you sorry? For looking after my little Chee-Chaw and feeding him many dollars worth of bananas in your nice safe barn? Besides,

I almost liked losing Chee-Chaw just to have the big joy of getting him back!"

Then he looked at the boys very hard. "Look," he said. "I want to do something wonderful for you boys to say thank you for what you have done. Think of something that you want very, very much."

The boys went into another room and thought hard, while everyone else was drinking lemonade in the kitchen. Finally they returned. "We've decided," they said.

"What? What?" cried Mr. Antonio, clapping his hands. "Anything! I will make it happen before you can say one, two, three!"

Duff was the one to speak. "We'd like two free tickets for tomorrow's performance, so we can see Mulligan — no, Chee-Chaw — do his act."

"But the second thing is harder," said Simon.

"Yes," said Duff. "We want to keep Chee-Chaw long enough to take him to school tomorrow morning for show-and-tell."

Simon's black eyes were snapping. "Can we?" he begged. "*Please*."

"I can do better than that!" boomed Mr. Antonio. "I'll bring two of my best monkeys along too, and we'll give that class the best show-and-tell they ever saw!"

Before going to bed, the Dooleys all went out to the barn one last time.

"Mulligan!" called Duff. "Chee-Chaw! Showtime! Come down and see my family again."

The monkey sailed down from the roof and landed softly on the rocking chair. He looked around, scratched his chest thoughtfully, and shook hands with everybody.

"Oh, Duff!" said Mrs. Dooley, giving him a big hug. "I feel so guilty about not believing you."

"Sorry, son," said Mr. Dooley.

"Me too," said Eileen.

"That's okay," said Duff. "With all the space aliens and

alligators in our house, I can understand your problem.
Still — I'm really glad it's all fixed up now."

Then they all said goodnight to Mulligan-Chee-Chaw, and went to bed.

7
Show and tell

The next morning, the monkeys and Mr. Antonio and Duff and Simon arrived at school half-an-hour before the bell rang. Duff took Mr. Antonio to the first-aid room, and told him he wouldn't be disturbed until it was time for show-and-tell. Then he rushed off to his homeroom for roll call.

The time before show-and-tell seemed like forever. There was a math class, followed by a spelling test. Duff spelled twenty of the forty words wrong. After that, there was silent reading, and it was almost impossible to sit still. Then came fifteen long minutes of writing.

At last Mrs. Huppman said, "All right, class. It's time for show-and-tell. If anyone wants first turn, raise your hand."

Duff's arm shot up like a rocket. "Fine, Duff," said the teacher. "Put your books away and come up to the front of the room. When everyone is settled down, we'll start."

Simon had already slipped out the rear classroom door and raced down to the first aid room. By the time Duff reached Mrs. Huppman's desk, everyone could hear scuffles and squeaks out in the hall. Facing the class, Duff said, "I want you all to meet Mulligan, otherwise known as Chee-Chaw, and two of his friends." The door opened.

While Mr. Antonio played a march on his harmonica, the three monkeys entered the room. They wore their red monkey suits, and did a fancy little step-hop as they came in. Every time Mulligan-Chee-Chaw did something new, the others did the same thing. They galloped around the room as though they were riding horses. They leapt from desk to desk, and hung

from the top edge of the chalkboard.

Mulligan jumped up on Mrs. Huppman's shoulder as the other monkeys did a dance around her. The children clapped and clapped, and then Mulligan-Chee-Chaw dashed over and sat on Duff's lap and gave him a hug. The other two monkeys went and sat on top of Simon's desk, and let him try on their hats and pat their heads.

Finally, Mr. Antonio passed around a giant bunch of bananas, and the class had a banana party.

Mrs. Huppman rose and called the class to order. "I think we all owe Duff and Simon an apology," she said.

"We refused to believe them about the monkey in the barn, and now we know it was all true. Duff, Simon, we're very sorry."

"Oh, that's okay, Mrs. Huppman," grinned Duff. "If someone told me they had a monkey over at their house, I wouldn't believe it either. Especially if it was someone who was always talking about sea serpents and dragons."

Then it was Mr. Antonio's turn for a speech. "Now it is time for us to be leaving. As a special thankyou to the boys, I'm giving them a circus pass. That means that they can go to the circus anytime, anywhere we raise our big tent. Then they'll be

able to see their special
monkey friend do his act,
many, many times. And to
this great bunch of kids, I
give a big invitation. I want
you to come to the circus
Saturday afternoon, free of
charge, to see what a great
act our monkeys can perform,
now that my Chee-Chaw is
back to lead them."

The kids clapped and
cheered, and then Mr.
Antonio and his monkeys left.

8
No more monkey business

After the performance on Saturday, Duff and Simon went into the animal tent to say goodbye to Mulligan-Chee-Chaw. Duff gave him an extra large and perfect banana, which he had stuffed in his pocket. "Thank you for coming to stay with us for a while," he said. "See ya next year."

Simon could feel a tear gathering at the corner of his eye. "Don't forget us," he whispered to Mulligan, and gave him a hug. Duff and

Simon waved as they turned the corner onto Lansdowne Street, and the monkey waved back.

"Know what, Duff?" sighed Simon, as they got closer to home. "I feel real bad. I feel like I've lost one of my best friends."

"Me too," said Duff, in a husky voice. "One thing I know for sure. If we live to be a hundred years old, we'll never, ever have a real monkey in our barn again."

They walked along in silence for a while. Then Duff spoke. "The thing to do is think of something cheerful." But they couldn't come up with one single cheerful thought.

Duff picked up a rock and tried to hit a lamp post. "Missed," he said gloomily.

Simon kicked an old Coke tin along the sidewalk till he

stubbed his toe on a curb. "Drat it!" he yelled. "Everything's awful!"

Then Duff started to smile.

"What is it?" asked Simon. "Tell me."

"Well," said Duff. "I was thinking of all those circuses we're going to see. And for free. And of how famous we're going to be in school next week. And how good it made me feel, right in the pit of my stomach, to hear all those people saying they were sorry. But ..."

"But what?" said Simon.

"Mostly," said Duff, as he shoved his fingers through his wild red hair, "I was thinking of what I'm going to do with my allowance this week."

"What?" asked Simon.

"*Spend it*!" shouted Duff, jumping over Mrs. LeBlanc's big rose bush.

"*And not on bananas*!" yelled Simon.

"Right on!" said Duff. "Hey, Simon! Race you home! Betcha I can beat you four times over!"

"Bet you can't!" yelled Simon, as they started up Sherbrooke Street. "Hey, Simon," panted Duff, as they raced along, "let's spend the time before supper looking for stray spacemen who've fallen out of their saucers! Okay by you?"

"Okay by me!" said Simon.

And that's exactly what they did.

Meet all the great kids in the First Novels Series!